Text © 1996 by Brian Heinz
Illustrations © 1996 by Jon Van Zyle
All rights reserved.

Typeset in Truesdell.
Type design by Laura Jane Coats
and Suellen Ehnebuske.
Printed in Hong Kong.

The paintings in this book were
rendered in acrylic on masonite board.

Library of Congress
Cataloging-in-Publication Data:
Heinz, Brian J., 1946-
Kayuktuk: An Arctic Quest/
by Brian J. Heinz;
illustrated by Jon Van Zyle.
p.   cm.

Summary: Young Aknik must
prove to his tribe that he can hunt
before he is accepted as a man.

ISBN 0-8118-0411-9
[1. Arctic regions – Fiction.]
I. Van Zyle, Jon, ill. II. Title.
PZ7.H36855Ki 1996
[Fic] – dc20 94-44526
CIP   AC

Distributed in Canada
by Raincoast Books
8680 Cambie Street,
Vancouver B.C. V6P 6M9

Distributed in Australia
and New Zealand
by CIS Cardigan Street
245-249 Cardigan Street
Carlton 3053 Australia

10 9 8 7 6 5 4 3 2 1

Chronicle Books
275 Fifth Street
San Francisco, CA 94103

For Bill Fix, who first introduced me to his Arctic fox Kayuktuk,
and for Ron Jobe, my mentor at Chautauqua.

B. J. H.

For all my eskimo friends, thank you for sharing
your inua with me, Kuyanak.

J. V. Z.

Acknowledgement must be given to Mr. G. Tieman,
librarian at the Chugiak-Eagle River Branch Library, for providing
the author with a copy of the Inupiat Eskimo Dictionary
by Donald H. Webster and Wilfried Zibell,
Summer Institute of Linguistics, Fairbanks, Alaska, 1970.

B. J. H.

Special thanks to John Trent, Howard Green, and
Craig George 'fur' their Arctic fox help...

J. V. Z.

Kayuktuk

AN ARCTIC QUEST

by BRIAN HEINZ

illustrations by JON VAN ZYLE

chronicle books · san francisco

Aknik approached his bird snare hopefully. "This time I will make Father proud," he whispered. "This time, I will show them all." His heartbeats quickened, but he feared what he would find.

The young hunter fell to his knees in the boggy tundra moss and studied the trap. "*Piitchuk,*" he muttered. "Empty again." Aknik slammed his fist down and ground his knuckles into the earth. What will I tell the camp today? he wondered. How will I return with pride? He took a deep breath and drove the painful thoughts from his mind.

Aknik read the ground signs. Scattered white feathers were caught in the tiny Arctic willows hugging the earth nearby. Dots of fresh blood stained the mossy rocks and Aknik knew the story.

"My trap was good!" he shouted to the wind. "I have caught an *akargik*. And for the third time my ptarmigan has been stolen!"

From the signs, Aknik knew the thief had left only moments ago. Yet, as before, there were no tracks to follow. It was spring, but the earth was still firm in winter's grip.

Aknik rose to his feet and clutched his spear. Turning slowly, he scanned the *natiġnak*, the flat tundra surrounding him. The landscape was laced with shallow creeks and ponds filling with the first spring melt. Patches of snow embraced low mounds of marsh grasses and saxifrage. In the distance, dark rocky crags reached upward and pointed to the open Bering Sea beyond.

For a fleeting instant, Aknik's sharp eyes fixed on a moving smudge of gray that whisked across the glacial ice and faded away. A shadow, he thought. Just a shadow. Aknik reset the snare and made the long walk back to the camp of tents.

Aknik's older sister, Aylette, worked on seal pelts stretched across a wooden frame. The curved blade of her *ulu* whispered across the skin in broad strokes. Mother was splitting whitefish nearby. The women looked up briefly at Aknik and nodded a greeting. They did not speak, or smile, but continued to work.

Aknik knew their thoughts. My hunting bag is empty again. That is what is in their minds.

Aknik stared at the ground and moved awkwardly on to the center of camp. A group of older boys suddenly appeared in front of him and blocked his path. They were grinning and Aknik braced himself for their words.

"Look!" shouted the tallest boy. "Aknik, the mighty hunter, has returned. And do you know what he has captured to feed our people today?"

"Tell us! Tell us!" teased the others.

The tall boy puffed out his chest proudly and placed his hands like a chief on Aknik's shoulders. In a solemn voice, he stated, "He has trapped . . . a bag of air to share with us."

The group of boys exploded in laughter. Their pointing fingers were like dull knives deep in Aknik's heart. His cheeks flushed red with heat, but Aknik stood firm. "I have told you all before what happened," he said slowly.

"Oh, yes," taunted another boy. "Your traps are robbed by *piiṇiḷaḳ* — ghosts who leave no signs. How could we forget?" The boys broke into laughter again.

Aknik stumbled past them and blinked away the wetness in his eyes. But a taunting voice shouted after him, "There goes mighty Aknik, the hunter who brings back only ghost stories for his people!"

Aknik approached his family's *tupiḳ*. The large skin tent stood at the edge of the encampment set up for the first spring hunt. His father and brother worked with other hunters to load the *umiaḳ*. The men and their sturdy boat would soon be pounding into the sea in search of the bowhead whales.

Aknik watched his brother thrust and twist a lance into an imaginary whale, a mound of snow. Aknik's heart throbbed. He quivered with excitement and blurted out, "I can hunt the whale, too. Will you take me, Father?"

All the men grew silent. Aknik's father stepped forward and clutched the sack tied around Aknik's waist. He shook it and stared at his youngest son. "You want to hunt the *ạgvik*?" he asked firmly. "First, you must prove yourself worthy. And you can not do that with an empty bag."

Aknik ducked into his tent to escape the eyes of the men. He heard the boat sliding lightly across the ice to the water's edge. He listened until the sounds of the paddles beating the waves faded away.

The tent flap opened slowly and a stout figure wrapped in bearskins stepped inside. Aknik looked up and into the face of Ticasuk, the Shaman.

The old man spoke. "You are having some trouble in proving your manhood, Aknik?"

The boy wiped his eyes and nodded. "I am a fine hunter. But they will not believe me. Each day, the birds in my snare are taken. It must be a *piinilak*, a phantom. The thief leaves no tracks."

"Did you truly see nothing?" The Shaman spoke slowly. "Think."

"I saw only a shadow . . . moving in the distance. Nothing else."

"Listen to me," the Shaman said. "Maybe your thief is real. Perhaps it is Kayuktuk, the Shadow Without a Body. You must discover the true nature of Kayuktuk. And you must bring proof to the village. Then you will have respect."

"But how can I catch a shadow? Will you summon the spirits to guide me? Will you make powerful magic to help me?" begged Aknik.

"No," replied the Shaman. "Courage must be your spirit. Wisdom must be your magic. The power must come from you." With those words, Ticasuk was gone.

Aknik did not sleep that night. The Shaman's words echoed in his head. He knew what he must do.

In the hours before dawn, Aknik stole from his blankets and lit the wick of the *nanik̦*. The soapstone lamp cast a soft glow as the seal oil burned with a low, yellow flame. The family slept soundly.

Aknik slipped into his leggings and parka. He padded the inside soles of his mukluks with soft, dry moss for warmth and pulled the boots onto his feet. He fingered a handful of tasty salmonberry *akutuk̦* into his mouth and placed a chunk of dried caribou in his hunting sack. He took up his spear and stepped out into the dim arctic light.

The flickering green dance of the northern lights faded under a low sun as Aknik arrived at the snare. Great clouds stormed in from the sea carried by a fierce wind. New snow swirled dizzily down. Aknik placed the dried meat in the center of the snarl and curled up behind a thick hummock of grass nearby to wait. "Here is your meat, my phantom," Aknik whispered. "I wait for you, Kayuktuk. Step into my snare. Let me see the shadow that steals."

Aknik waited. He watched . . . and he waited. Fear crept into his mind. And he wondered . . . What use is a spear against a ghost?

He huddled against the stinging cold. Still he waited. This time, no matter what, Aknik thought, I will return as a hunter or I will not return at all. But he grew tired. His eyes drooped and closed. Soon, Aknik lay under a thin blanket of white.

A scratching sound roused Aknik from his half-sleep. He peered through the grass at the snare. Empty! He raced to the trap and studied the ground. Small prints were patterned in the new snow. "You are real!" Aknik shouted. His eyes followed the path far out onto the tundra.

Through the falling snow, he spied a small, gray shape racing away. With spear in hand, Aknik charged after it. The fleeting ghost disappeared. Aknik trained his eyes on the tracks in front of him. If he were not quick, the snow would cover the trail. Excitement drove his young legs over outcroppings of rock and across rivulets. His heart pounded. He sucked in deep breaths of icy air. He loped for miles over the rolling tundra until his legs throbbed. Then, the trail stopped suddenly at the base of a mountain near the sea.

A small shelf of stone hung over a narrow opening in the rock. Aknik fell to his knees and peered into the dark crevice. Soft, rapid panting came from the tiny cave. A pair of small eyes flashed back at him. He raised his spear and demanded, "What are you?" As if to answer the question, Aknik's phantom stepped out into the light.

"A Fox," Aknik gasped. "So you are Kayuktuk, the Shadow Without a Body." The fox stood motionless before him. The thick fur rippled in the wind. Aknik could see how perfectly the fox was masked in the gray colors of the land. Short, delicate legs stood on small fur-covered paws. He understood why the fox rarely left its mark on the ground and why it was given away only by its shadow in the sun. And he admired the cunning of his thief.

Then, Aknik remembered his purpose. He drew back his arm, steadied his spear, and aimed at where he believed the fox's heart to be.

A series of muted whimpers and yips caused the fox to turn away into the darkness. Aknik dropped his weapon. He crawled forward. Six young kits scrambled for warm spots against their mother's belly.

"So, Kayuktuk," said Aknik, "you are Mother Fox with good reason for robbing my trap."

The fox looked into Aknik's eyes and growled softly. There was no fear in her face. Silently, they faced each other for a long time.

Aknik spoke softly, "I could kill you, Kayuktuk, and your six whelps would perish. Who would care? Who would know? I must prove I have faced you." Aknik argued with himself and, finally, knew he could not take the fox's spirit from her. But Ticasuk, the Shaman, had told him to bring proof of Kayuktuk to the village.

Aknik thought. He slipped the *aggiññak* from his shoulder. The hunting bag was stiff with cold. Carefully, he reached down and filled the skin bag. Then, Aknik gently raised the bag back onto his shoulder and took up his spear.

Aknik returned to camp late, guided by
the shimmering glow of blazing campfires and the
singing of songs. The voices died out in silence as
Aknik entered the circle of tents. All eyes were on
his hunting bag. Aknik studied the crowd. There . . .
the group of boys who had tormented him. And
there, his family and the hope they held in their eyes.
Finally, he saw Ticasuk, the Shaman. The old man
stepped forward. "Have you brought us Kayuktuk?"

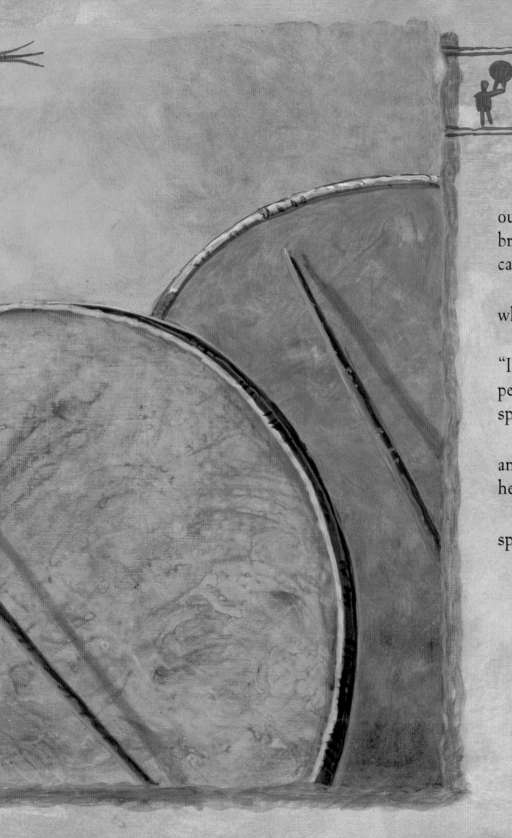

Aknik held open his bag. The Shaman lifted out a frozen handful of snow and smiled. Murmurs broke out in the crowd as they moved in closer. There, captured in the snow, was the fox's print for all to see.

"You have done well," said the Shaman, "but why did you not bring us the pelt of Kayuktuk?"

Aknik stood tall and spoke with confidence. "I might have one pelt now, or there may be many pelts in the fall." Then Aknik told his tale and all spoke of his wisdom and his courage.

Aknik's father stepped from the crowd and faced his son. "Tomorrow we hunt the whale," he said proudly.

The drums began to beat. Aknik raised his spear and danced.

A NOTE FROM THE AUTHOR

For thousands of years, the cold, and sometimes savage, environment of the Arctic has been home to the Iñupiat, the native people sometimes called "Eskimos." The Iñupiat are a proud and courageous people with a unique culture rich in story, dance, song, and art.

This is a "coming-of-age" tale about Aknik, an Iñupiat boy. The story takes place in northwestern Alaska at a time when the Iñupiat lived in traditional ways, when the land and sea fulfilled all their needs and before the coming of modern conveniences that are common to their culture today.

There are many languages and dialects in the varied nations of the Iñupiat. The native words used in this story are based on the Iñupiat Eskimo Dictionary by Donald H. Webster and Wilfried Zibell, published by the 1970 Summer Institute of Linguistics, Inc., Box 1028, Fairbanks, Alaska, 99701.

GLOSSARY

aġġiññak (ah · gĭn´· yahk) a storage bag, hunting sack, or knapsack.

aġvik (ahg´· vĭk) bowhead whale, a species specifically found in Arctic waters and traditionally hunted by Arctic peoples.

akargik (ah · kar´· gĭk) the willow ptarmigan, a bird native to the Arctic; the willow ptarmigan is the state bird of Alaska.

akutuk (ah´· kŭ · tŭk) a food of cooked fats, meats, and berries.

Iñupiat (ĭn · yōō´· pē · ŭt´) a language spoken by the indigenous people of north and northwest Alaska; the language spoken by the Iñupiat.

kayuktuk (kah · yŏŏk´· tŏŏk) fox. Both the red fox and the arctic fox are found in Alaska and there are a variety of native words in different dialects to name them.

The fox described in this book is the Arctic fox.

nanik (nŭn´· ĭk) an oil lamp, usually shaped from soft stone, with a wick of dried moss.

natiġnak (nŭ´· tĭg · nahk) the flat tundra of the Arctic environment.

piiṇilak (pēē´· nē · lahk) a ghost, or the spirit of one who has died.

piitchuk (pēēt´· chŏŏk) empty, nothing.

tupik (tōō´· pik) tent or house.

ulu (ōō´· lōō) a woman's knife with a curved blade for scraping hides.

umiak (ōō´· mē · ahk) a large skin boat capable of holding 8 to 10 men, and traditionally used in the hunting of whales.